PHOTOGRAPHY BY ANN CUTTING | DESIGN & ALLITERATIONS BY VALERIE GATES

The Alphabet of Bugs

An ABC Book

Sky Pony Press
New York

Ailanthus Webworm Moth artfully alights Amber

Bess Beetle balances Bittersweet background

C

Chrysina counterbalances charming Capri color

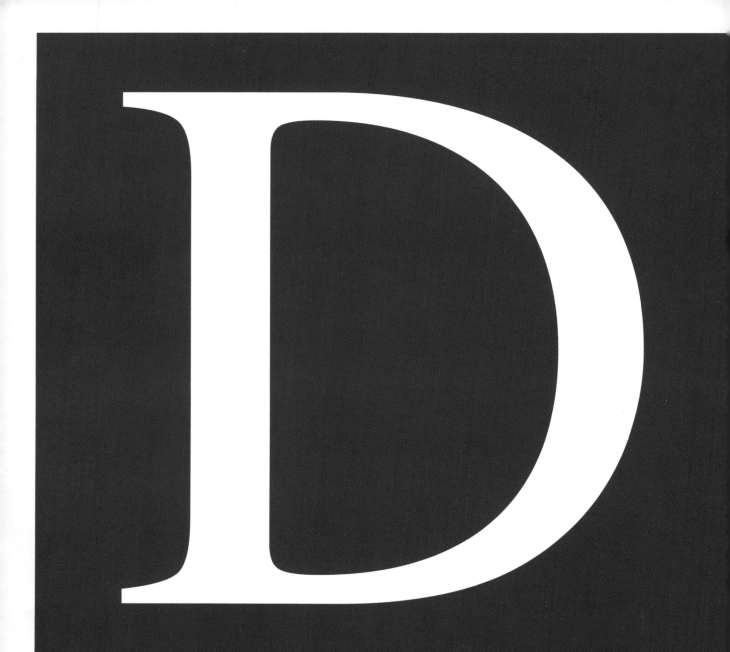

Dog Day Cicada displays Denim dashingly

E

Eastern Lubber Grasshopper enhances Emerald effect

Flatid Leaf Bug flaunts flawless Flax facade

G

Giant Leaf Insect graces Glaucous glow

Hawk Moth harmonizes hip Honeydew hue

I

Ironclad Beetle integrates Iris iridescence

J

Japanese Beetle jauntily justifies jeweled Jade

K

Katydid keenly kicks Keppel

Lantern Fly likes Lilac luster

M

Mason Wasp magnificently mimics Moccasin

Net-winged Beetle nestles neatly near Nyanza

O

Owl Butterfly operates optimally on Ochra

P

Pharaoh Cicada perfectly pairs pretty Peridot

Q

Question Mark Butterfly quells Quinacridone Magenta

Rhinoceros Beetle relishes regal Rackley

Sphinx Moth savors Salmon surroundings

T

Tarantula Hawk transforms tasteful Thistle tone

U

Ulysses Butterfly unveils ultra underlay upon Ube

V

Velvet Ant vitalizes vague Vanilla vector

Weevil waits winsomely within Wheat

Xyleutes Moth x-ing Xanthic xanadu

Y

Yellow Umbrella Stick Insect yields Yellow yard

Zebra Longwing Butterfly zips Zomp

Boston-based Art Director Valerie Gates teams up again with her friend photographer Ann Cutting to create this second book in the series that introduces some funky bugs on more lesser-known colors. Valerie's favorite bug in the book is the Katydid because it looks like a ballet dancer. Ann lives in Pasadena and her favorite bug in the book is the Question Mark Butterfly because it has a question mark on the underside of its wings.

The authors would like to thank the good folks at Bioquip Products and Bioquip bugs for their help and expertise. Special thanks to Celia, Brent, and Chris. Visit www.bioquip.com.

The Alphabet of Bugs "Did You Know...?" Glossary:

Ailanthus Webworm Moth is often mistaken for a beetle because of its bright coloring.

Bess Beetles can produce fourteen distinct acoustical signals to communicate with their colonies.

Chrysina is also known as a Jewel Scarab.

Dog Day Cicada taps into trees with its beak to feed.

Eastern Lubbers are quite clumsy, can't fly, and mostly walk or crawl feebly to get around.

Flatid Leaf Bugs are native to Madagascar and begin life looking like wispy white feathers.

Giant Leaf Insects can be parthenogenetic—lay unfertilized eggs, which give rise only to new females.

Hawk Moths are named for their hovering, swift flight patterns.

Ironclad Beetles play dead so well that jewelers in Mexico decorate and sell them as living bling.

Japanese Beetles are clumsy flyers and drop several centimeters when they hit a wall.

Katydids rub their forewings together to create their signature "katy-did, katy-didn't" call.

Lantern Flies' long snouts scare off predators—but they don't really glow.

Mason Wasps build their nests with "mud" made from earth and regurgitated water.

Net-winged Beetles are protected from predators by being toxic.

Owl Butterflies are very large and can have a wingspan eight inches wide.

Pharaoh Cicadas spend most of their thirteen- or seventeen-year lives underground.

Question Mark Butterflies feed on fermenting fruit and can appear to be intoxicated.

Rhinoceros Beetles are kept as pets in Asia, and the males are gambled on in fighting matches.

Sphinx Moths are known for their rapid, sustained flying ability.

Tarantula Hawks hunt spiders and tarantulas as food for their larvae.

Ulysses Butterfly can be seen as a sudden bright blue flash from hundreds of meters away.

Velvet Ants are really wingless wasps and make a high-pitched squeaking sound when disturbed.

Weevils come from a large family of beetles and are known for their distinctively shaped snout.

Xyleutes are considered forestry pests and bore through the trunks and branches of trees.

Yellow Umbrella Stick Insects are very popular to frame and hang on the wall as decoration.

Zebra Longwing Butterflies roost in large groups and return to the same roost every night.

Copyright Page Images: Lime Swallowtail (L), Majestic Green Swallowtail (R)